Are You Thinking Again, Dear?

Are You Thinking Again, Dear?

By ALIKI

With thanks to the Hudson River School of Music

Bibliographical Note

Are You Thinking Again, Dear? is a new work, first published by Dover
Publications, Inc., in 2018.

Library of Congress Cataloging-in-Publication Data

Names: Aliki, author, illustrator.
Title: Are you thinking again, dear? / written and illustrated by Aliki.
Description: Mineola, New York. : Dover Publications, Inc., 2018. | Summary:
    Charles's habit of getting lost in his thoughts rather than doing what he
    should continually gets him in trouble at home and in school.
Identifiers: LCCN 2017020846| ISBN 9780486819549 | ISBN 048681954X
Subjects: | CYAC: Thought and thinking—Fiction. | Mindfulness
    (Psychology)—Fiction. | Schools—Fiction. | Family life—Fiction. |
    Behavior—Fiction.
Classification: LCC PZ7.A397 Are 2018 | DDC [E]—dc23
LC record available at https://lccn.loc.gov/2017020846

Manufactured in China by RR Donnelley
81954X01   2018
www.doverpublications.com

For Estella Polaris
my Star

"Charles!" called Mother.

"You'll be late for school again!"

When Charles finally appeared, Mother sighed.

"Now what's wrong with that picture?"

Charles took a look at himself.

"I found my wings," said Charles. "You told me to hurry."

"Today is not Halloween," said Mother.

"I found Marsha's wings, too, so we can hurry together."

Mother took a deep breath.

"Charles, dear, if only you would think about
what you should be thinking about."

Charles sat at the table to eat his Crunchies.
"It would be easier with a spoon, dear," said Mother.
But Charles was thinking about Niagara Falls.

After breakfast, Charles brushed his teeth,
pulled on his backpack, and left for school.
"Mind where you walk, dear," said Mother.
"Look left, look right, and straight ahead."
"I will," said Charles.

It was a breezy day.

Seed pods whirled down like helicopters.

Charles collected some, and stuck one on his nose.

He was thinking about his new nose.

That's why he bumped into a tree.

At school, Nurse Dilly bandaged Charles.

"Thank you, Nurse Dilly," he said.

"Here's a nose for you."

Miss Crocky took attendance.
"Congratulations, girls and boys.
No one is absent. You are all present!"

"Spelling time," said Miss Crocky.

She wrote c-a-t on the board.

Charles raised his hand.

"Miss Crocky, my pencil doesn't write."

"They were all sharpened this morning,"
said Miss Crocky.

Charles took a closer look.

"Oops," he laughed.

"Maybe if I turned it around it would."

The children giggled.

They thought Charles was funny.

But Miss Crocky didn't.

Charles was disrupting the class again.

After recess, Miss Crocky took out the math sheets.
The children did their numbers.
But Charles was thinking of the glider he wanted to make.
The math sheet was just the right size.

Charles was ready for the test flight
when Miss Crocky noticed him.
"CHARLES! WHAT ARE YOU..."

"Success!" cried Charles.
The glider made a perfect landing.
The class gave a roar!

"I've had enough," said Miss Crocky.
"Go straight to Mr. Mickle's office."
Charles knew where it was.
He had been there before.

"What is it this time, Charles?" asked Mr. Mickle.
"Well, Mr. Mickle, I saw the math sheet
and it gave me a good idea..."
"Ideas are great," said Mr. Mickle, "except math is thinking
about numbers, not about aeronautics."

"Charles," said Mr. Mickle kindly,
"sometimes you are ABSENT-minded.
What you want is to be PRESENT-minded.
Just sit here awhile and think about that."
Charles took a seat.

It was lunchtime.

"Buenos días, Carlos," said Pedro, eating his pizza.

"Buen apetito, Pedro," said Charles, opening his lunch box.

"Caramba! My favorite. Peanut butter on rye.
What do you have, Pedro?"

"I already had it," said Pedro, taking his last bite.

Charles was wondering if the peanut butter would stick
to the roof of his mouth when the bell rang.

"They never give you enough time to eat in this school," he said.

"Not if you're dreaming," said Pedro.

And off Pedro went to violin practice.

"What?" said Father. "Another phone call from Miss Crocky?
Another visit to Mr. Mickle's office!" His tail rattled.
"That boy is always thinking about what he's not doing!
A Timeout is what I got when I did that," said Father.
"Let's be patient," said Mother.
"In other ways, Charles is such a dear child.
He is thoughtful, funny, kind to animals,
and he never forgets his 'thank you.'
Remember when he was little and ate all those things
he shouldn't? He got over that, didn't he?"

But Father was worried.
"I can't wait that long," he said.
"He might do something dangerous.
Like dive into an empty swimming pool.
I almost did that once."

Charles was setting the table with Marsha.
"Maybe we'll feel better after dinner," Father said.

But after they read to their children,
and tucked them in bed, Father was still worried.
He was thinking hard. He was making plans.

The next day Father took Charles to the doctor.

"Charles is fit and vitamin-sufficient," pronounced the doctor.

He took Charles to the dentist.

"Perfect teeth. No toothache in sight!" said the dentist.

"Let's celebrate," said Father as they passed the playground.

"That was fun," said Father.
"We make a good team," said Charles.

"You're late," said Mother.
"Wash up, boys. Dinner is on the table."
Mother and Marsha waited.

And waited.

But Father and Charles were busy.

"What took you so long?" said Mother.

"We did what you told us to do," said Charles.

"We washed up."

Poor Charles. He tried ways to focus on what he was doing.

The signs didn't always help.

When Mother asked him to put his blocks away, he did.

But he was always thinking about something else.

Mother was running out of patience when the doorbell rang.
Charles's hero, Great Uncle Crocódila! What a surprise!
They had not seen Great Uncle Crocódila for a long time.
How did such a famous scientist find time to visit?
They celebrated with tea and cookies.

"You both look pale," said Great Uncle Crocódila.

"Is something troubling you?"

"Well, it's just..." started Mother.

"It's Charles," said Father, and told his sad story.

"You do have a problem," said Great Uncle solemnly.

"It IS a problem to be a thinker."

"No, but..." said Mother.

"An empty head would be better," said Great Uncle.

"Or marbles instead of brains."

"No, but..." said Father.

"My dears, Thinkers think," said famous Great Uncle Crocódila.
"There's a little pot on a stove up there cooking up thoughts.
When the thoughts are done, the cooking is finished.
Would you turn off your oatmeal before it's ready?"

Just then Charles walked in with a big hug for Great Uncle Crocódila.

"Ahhh, here's the boy I've been hearing about," he said kindly.

"Did I hear oatmeal?" asked Charles.

Great Uncle laughed.

"We were just saying that thinking is like cooking.

You keep your mind on the front burner until the oatmeal is done.

And then you go to the next burner."

"Oh!" said Charles with an excited jump.
"You have to stay *Present!*
That's what Mr. Mickle said."

"What did Mr. Mickle say?" asked Father in surprise.

"Mr. Mickle said I am *Absent*-minded," said Charles.

"I have to be more *Present*-minded."

"Exactly!" said Great Uncle.

"Brilliant, Charles! And brilliant, Mr. Mickle."

"Bingo!" said Father. "Now you're cooking, my boy!"

"No pot will burn here," laughed Mother.

"I see you make gliders," said Great Uncle.

"Let's all take a nice walk and talk aeronautics."

"And gliders and helicopters. And wings," said Charles.

"And birdies," said Marsha.

Great Uncle Crocódila took his hat and cane.

"Is that the way you carry your cane?" Charles asked.

"Oh no," laughed Great Uncle.

"I was just thinking of something else."

When they were gone, Father said,

"Does Great Uncle remind you of someone?"

"Yes," laughed Mother.

"Thinkers seem to run in the family."